KALOS
BEGINNER'S HANDBOOK

POKéMON
Gotta catch 'em all! ™

KALOS
BEGINNER'S HANDBOOK

SCHOLASTIC INC.

ISBN 978-0-545-64396-2

12 11 10 9 8 7 6 5 4 3 2 1   14 15 16 17 18 19/0

Designed by Two Red Shoes Design Inc.

Printed in the U.S.A.   40

First printing, January 2014

CONTENTS

WELCOME TO THE KALOS REGION

Welcome to the beautiful Kalos region! This is where all your incredible new Pokémon battles will unfold. Kalos is the perfect place for a Pokémon Trainer to shine!

Before you start your journey, you need to know the lay of the land. Use this book as your guide. There is so much fun to be had in Kalos, especially if you know where to look. There are plenty more places to explore. Get ready for the journey of a lifetime!

HOW TO USE THIS BOOK

Here are the basics you'll discover about each Pokémon:

HOW TO SAY IT

When it comes to Pokémon pronunciation, it's easy to get tongue-tied! There are many Pokémon with unusual names, but we're here to help you sound them out. Our guide will have you saying Pokémon names so perfectly that you'll sound like a professor!

HEIGHT AND WEIGHT

How does each Pokémon measure up? Find out by checking its height and weight stats. And remember, good things can come in small packages — or in any size and shape. It's up to every Trainer to work with his/her Pokémon pal and play up its size.

POSSIBLE MOVES

Every Pokémon has its own unique combination of moves. Before you hit the battlefield, we'll tell you all about each Pokémon's awesome attacks. And don't forget, with a good Trainer, they can always learn more!

DESCRIPTION

Knowledge is power! Pokémon Trainers have to know their stuff. Find out everything you've ever wanted to know about the new Pokémon here.

TYPE

Each Pokémon has a type, and some even have two! (Pokémon with two types are called dual-type Pokémon.) Every type of Pokémon comes with its advantages and disadvantages. We'll break them all down for you here.

Curious about what Pokémon types you can spot in Kalos? Find out about all eighteen (yes, there's a brand-new one!) by turning the page. . . .

GUIDE TO POKÉMON TYPES

A Pokémon's type can tell you a lot about it. From clues about where to find it in the wild, to the moves it'll be able to use on the battlefield, type is the key to unlocking a Pokémon's power.

A clever Trainer always considers type advantage when picking a Pokémon for a match, because it shows a Pokémon's strengths and also its weaknesses. For example, a Fire-type may melt an Ice-type, but against a Water-type, it might find it's the one in hot water. And while a Water-type usually has the upper hand in battle with a Fire-type, a Water-type move would act like a sprinkler on a Grass-type. But when that same Grass-type is battling a Fire-type, it just might get scorched.

Keep in mind that moves can be mightier based on the location of the battle. Rock-type Pokémon rock at mountainside battles, Electric-types get charged up near power plants, and Ground-types like to get down and dirty right in the dirt. And if a Pokémon has two types—that is, if it's a dual-type—well, then it's double trouble!

Here are the eighteen different Pokémon types:

Fire

Grass

Water

Normal

Electric

Bug

Ghost

Flying

Fighting

Psychic

Steel

Rock

Ground

Ice

Poison

Dark

Dragon

Fairy

INTRODUCING THE NEW FAIRY-TYPE

In the beginning, there were only fifteen Pokémon types. Then came the discovery of the Dark- and Steel-types in the Johto region. Here in Kalos, another type has been unearthed—the Fairy-type! Be on the lookout for Fairy-types like Flabébé, Spritzee, Swirlix, Sylveon, and even the Legendary Pokémon Xerneas.

With the discovery of this new type, tons of new genetic information has been unlocked. This is exciting news—especially if you like Dragon-type battles! Fairy-type moves are particularly effective against Dragon-types, even when matched against powerful Pokémon like Salamence.

Pokémon researchers are scrambling to study this brand-new breed of Pokémon. The race is on to uncover everything about the mysterious Fairy-type. For now, just one thing's for sure—new Trainers are sure to learn a lot as they encounter this new type in Kalos!

MEET CHESPIN, FENNEKIN, AND FROAKIE

Every new Trainer gets their chance to pick out their first Pokémon—a Water-, Grass-, or Fire-type—from their regional research lab. In Kalos, Professor Sycamore helps Trainers start their journey at his lab in Vaniville Town. New Trainers can count on him for good advice and their pick of a great Pokémon pal! So read on to learn more about cool Chespin, furry Fennekin, and fun Froakie.

CHESPIN

FENNEKIN

FROAKIE

CHESPIN
Spiny Nut Pokémon

How to Say It: CHESS-pin

Height: 1' 04"

Weight: 19.8 lbs.

Possible Moves: Tackle, Growl, Vine Whip, Rollout, Bite, Leech Seed, Pin Missile, Take Down, Seed Bomb, Mud Shot, Bulk Up, Body Slam, Pain Split, Wood Hammer

TYPE:
GRASS

When Chespin flexes its soft quills, they become tough spikes with sharp, piercing points. It relies on its nutlike shell for protection in battle.

FENNEKIN

Fox Pokémon

How to Say It: FEN-ik-in

Height: 1' 04"

Weight: 20.7 lbs.

Possible Moves: Scratch, Tail Whip, Ember, Howl, Flame Charge, Psybeam, Fire Spin, Lucky Chant, Light Screen, Psyshock, Flamethrower, Will-O-Wisp, Psychic, Sunny Day, Magic Room, Fire Blast

TYPE:

FIRE

Searing heat radiates from Fennekin's large ears to keep opponents at a distance. It often snacks on twigs to gain energy.

FROAKIE

Bubble Frog Pokémon

How to Say It: FRO-kee

Height: 1′ 00″

Weight: 15.4 lbs.

Possible Moves: Pound, Growl, Bubble, Quick Attack, Lick, Water Pulse, Smokescreen, Round, Fling, Smack Down, Substitute, Bounce, Double Team, Hydro Pump

TYPE:
WATER

The foamy bubbles that cover Froakie's body protect its sensitive skin from damage. It's always alert to any changes in its environment.

MEET THE NEW LEGENDARY POKÉMON

Legendary Pokémon are rarely seen, but their strength is so unmistakable that when they do appear, you know you're in the presence of greatness. Each one is a force of nature. Spotting a Legendary Pokémon is an unforgettable experience, the kind of story Trainers tell their grand-children—that is, if they're lucky enough to see one!

Every region has its own Legendary Pokémon who help keep the universe in balance. In Kalos, that delicate harmony is created by Pokémon like Xerneas and Yveltal. They represent the circle of life.

YVELTAL

XERNEAS

XERNEAS
Life Pokémon

How to Say It: ZURR-nee-us

Height: 9′ 10″

Weight: 474.0 lbs.

Ability: Fairy Aura

Possible Moves: Heal Pulse, Aromatherapy, Ingrain, Take Down, Light Screen, Aurora Beam, Gravity, Geomancy, Moonblast, Megahorn, Night Slash, Horn Leech, Psych Up, Misty Terrain, Nature Power, Close Combat, Giga Impact, Outrage

TYPE:
FAIRY

Xerneas's horns shine in all the colors of the rainbow. It is said that this Legendary Pokémon can share the gift of endless life.

YVELTAL
Destruction Pokémon

How to Say It: ee-VELL-tall

Height: 19′ 00″

Weight: 447.5 lbs.

Ability: Dark Aura

Possible Moves: Hurricane, Razor Wind, Taunt, Roost, Double Team, Air Slash, Snarl, Oblivion Wing, Disable, Dark Pulse, Foul Play, Phantom Force, Psychic, Dragon Rush, Focus Blast, Sucker Punch, Hyper Beam, Sky Attack

TYPE:
DARK/
FLYING

When Yveltal spreads its dark wings, its feathers give off a red glow. It is said that this Legendary Pokémon can absorb the life energy of others.

EEVEE AND ITS EVOLUTIONS

In the Kalos region, you'll meet a new Evolution of Eevee—Sylveon! It's one of the first Fairy-type Pokémon discovered in Kalos.

Sylveon is Eevee's eighth Evolution. Turn the page to learn more about this amazing Pokémon and its fascinating forms.

EEVEE

ESPEON

FLAREON

GLACEON

JOLTEON

LEAFEON

SYLVEON

UMBREON

VAPOREON

EEVEE
Evolution Pokémon

How to Say It: EE-vee

Height: 1′ 00″

Weight: 14.3 lbs.

Possible Moves: Tackle, Tail Whip, Helping Hand, Sand Attack, Growl, Quick Attack, Bite, Baton Pass, Take Down, Last Resort, Trump Card

TYPE:
NORMAL

Behind Eevee's big brown eyes and cute fur collar lies an incredibly unique and mighty Pokémon. Because of its unusual genetic makeup, Eevee's DNA easily shifts, and it can evolve into many different types —eight that we know of so far! That's why Eevee is called the Evolution Pokémon.

SYLVEON
Intertwining Pokémon

How to Say It: SIL-vee-on

Height: 3′ 03″

Weight: 51.8 lbs.

Possible Moves: Disarming Voice, Tail Whip, Tackle, Helping Hand, Sand Attack, Fairy Wind, Quick Attack, Swift, Draining Kiss, Skill Swap, Misty Terrain, Light Screen, Moonblast, Last Resort, Psych Up

TYPE:
FAIRY

To keep others from fighting, Sylveon projects a calming aura from its feelers, which look like flowing ribbons. It wraps those ribbons around its Trainer's arm when they walk together.

VAPOREON

Bubble Jet Pokémon

How to Say It: vay-POR-ee-on

Height: 3′ 03″

Weight: 63.9 lbs.

While Vaporeon looks solid as a rock, its cell composition is actually so close to a molecule of H_2O that it can become one with a pool of water.

FLAREON

Flame Pokémon

TYPE: FIRE

How to Say It: FLARE-ae-on

Height: 2′ 11″

Weight: 55.1 lbs.

Flareon can use a flame sac in its body to raise its temperature to 1650° Fahrenheit!

JOLTEON
Lightning Pokémon

TYPE:
ELECTRIC

How to Say It: JOLT-ee-on

Height: 2' 07"

Weight: 54.0 lbs.

Jolteon can use its electricity like a blow dryer to straighten its fur. Then it sends electrical attacks from its fur directly at its foes.

ESPEON
Sun Pokémon

TYPE:
PSYCHIC

How to Say It: ESS-pee-on

Height: 2' 11"

Weight: 58.4 lbs.

No need to check the weather report when Espeon is around! Its fine fur can sense even the slightest shifts in the air and let you know if rain, sun, fog, or snow is on the way.

UMBREON

Moonlight Pokémon

TYPE:
DARK

How to Say It: UMM-bree-on

Height: 3' 03"

Weight: 59.5 lbs.

The moon's aura has a mighty and mysterious effect on Umbreon. The rings on its body begin to glow in the moonlight, signaling it has gained a magical strength.

GLACEON

Fresh Snow Pokémon

TYPE:
ICE

How to Say It: GLACE-ee-on

Height: 2' 07"

Weight: 57.1 lbs.

Glaceon can cool down its body temperature to create a snowy white storm from the air around it. This storm is so strong it can ice out an opponent.

LEAFEON

Verdant Pokémon

How to Say It: LEEF-ee-on

Height: 3′ 03″

Weight: 56.2 lbs.

TYPE:
GRASS

Leafeon is a nature lover, not a fighter. Like plants in the forest, the cells in its body power up with sunshine during a process called photosynthesis.

MEET OTHER NEW POKÉMON

A Pokémon with a sweet voice . . .
A Pokémon with a sweet tooth . . .
And plenty of Pokémon that are just
plain sweet. . . .

All these battling buddies and many
more live together in Kalos!

From Santalune to Lumiose City, Kalos
is a land full of wild and wonderful
Pokémon! Each new Pokémon has
an amazing Ability and an even more
amazing heart. And they're all waiting
to meet you! All you have to do is turn
the page. . . .

GOGOAT

FLETCHLING

HELIOPTILE

BUNNELBY

Digging Pokémon

How to Say It: BUN-ell-bee

Height: 1' 04"

Weight: 11.0 lbs.

Possible Moves: Tackle, Agility, Leer, Quick Attack, Double Slap, Mud-Slap, Take Down, Mud Shot, Double Kick, Odor Sleuth, Flail, Dig, Bounce, Super Fang, Facade, Earthquake

TYPE:
NORMAL

Bunnelby can use its ears like shovels to dig holes in the ground. Eventually, its ears become strong enough to cut through thick tree roots while it digs.

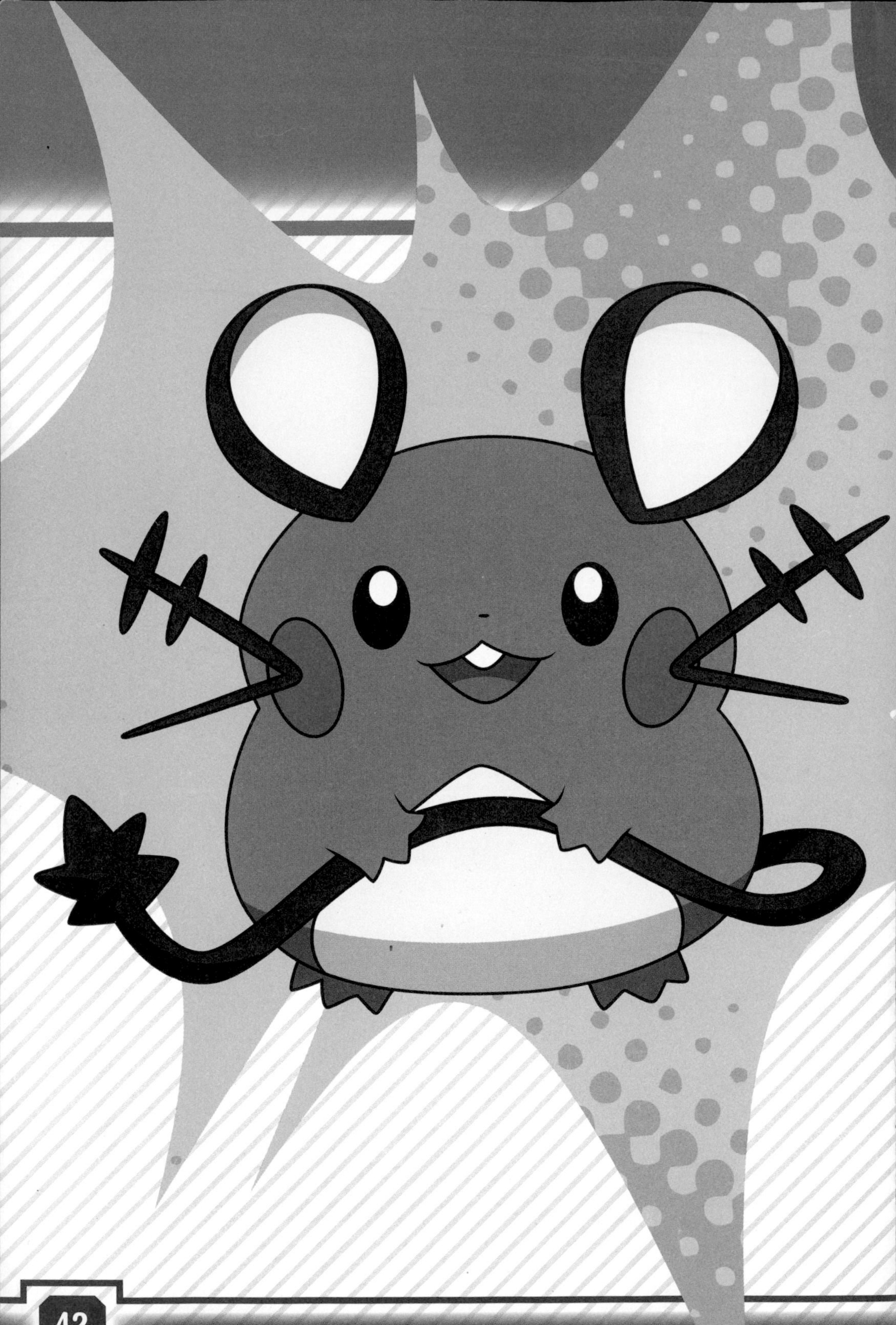

DEDENNE

Antenna Pokémon

How to Say It: deh-DEN-nay

Height: 0' 08"

Weight: 4.9 lbs.

Possible Moves: Tackle, Tail Whip, Thunder Shock, Charge, Charm, Parabolic Charge, Nuzzle, Thunder Wave, Volt Switch, Rest, Snore, Charge Beam, Entrainment, Play Rough, Thunder, Discharge

TYPE:
ELECTRIC/
FAIRY

Dedenne uses its whiskers like antennas to communicate over long distances using electrical waves. It can soak up electricity through its tail.

FLABÉBÉ

Single Bloom Pokémon

How to Say It: flah-BAY-BΛY

Height: 0′ 04″

Weight: 0.2 lbs.

Possible Moves: Tackle, Vine Whip, Fairy Wind,
Lucky Chant, Razor Leaf, Wish, Magical Leaf, Grassy Terrain,
Petal Blizzard, Aromatherapy, Misty Terrain, Moonblast,
Petal Dance, Solar Beam

TYPE:

FAIRY

Each Flabébé has a special connection with the flower it holds. They take care of their flowers and use them as an energy source.

FLETCHLING

Tiny Robin Pokémon

How to Say It: FLETCH-ling

Height: 1′ 00″

Weight: 3.7 lbs.

Possible Moves: Tackle, Growl, Quick Attack, Peck, Agility, Flail, Roost, Razor Wind, Natural Gift, Flame Charge, Acrobatics, Me First, Tailwind, Steel Wing

TYPE:
NORMAL/
FLYING

Flocks of Fletchling sing to one another in beautiful voices to communicate. If an intruder threatens their territory, they will defend it fiercely.

GOGOAT
Mount Pokémon

How to Say It: GO-goat

Height: 5' 07"

Weight: 200.6 lbs.

Possible Moves: Aerial Ace, Tackle, Growth, Vine Whip, Tail Whip, Leech Seed, Razor Leaf, Worry Seed, Synthesis, Take Down, Bulldoze, Seed Bomb, Bulk Up, Double-Edge, Horn Leech, Leaf Blade, Milk Drink, Earthquake

TYPE:
GRASS

This perceptive Pokémon can read its riders' feelings by paying attention to their grip on its horns. Gogoat also use their horns in battles for leadership.

HELIOPTILE
Generator Pokémon

How to Say It: hee-lee-AHP-tile

Height: 1′ 08″

Weight: 13.2 lbs.

Possible Moves: Pound, Tail Whip, Thunder Shock, Charge, Mud-Slap, Quick Attack, Razor Wind, Parabolic Charge, Thunder Wave, Bulldoze, Volt Switch, Electrify, Thunderbolt

TYPE:
ELECTRIC/
NORMAL

The frills on Helioptile's head soak up sunlight and create electricity. In this way, they can generate enough energy to keep them going without food.

INKAY

Revolving Pokémon

How to Say It: in-kay

Height: 1' 04"

Weight: 7.7 lbs.

Possible Moves: Tackle, Peck, Constrict, Reflect, Foul Play, Swagger, Psywave, Topsy-Turvy, Hypnosis, Psybeam, Switcheroo, Payback, Light Screen, Pluck, Psycho Cut, Slash, Night Slash, Superpower

TYPE:
DARK/
PSYCHIC

The spots on Inkay's body emit a flashing light. This light confuses its opponents, giving it a chance to escape.

LITLEO

Lion Cub Pokémon

How to Say It: LIT-lee-oh

Height: 2′ 00″

Weight: 29.8 lbs.

Possible Moves: Tackle, Leer, Ember, Work Up, Headbutt, Noble Roar, Take Down, Fire Fang, Endeavor, Echoed Voice, Flamethrower, Crunch, Hyper Voice, Incinerate, Overheat

TYPE:
FIRE/
NORMAL

When Litleo is ready to get stronger, it leaves its pride to live alone. During a battle, its mane radiates intense heat.

PANCHAM
Playful Pokémon

How to Say It: PAN-chum

Height: 2' 00"

Weight: 17.6 lbs.

Possible Moves: Tackle, Leer, Arm Thrust, Work Up, Karate Chop, Comet Punch, Slash, Circle Throw, Vital Throw, Body Slam, Crunch, Entrainment, Parting Shot, Sky Uppercut

TYPE:
FIGHTING

Pancham tries to be intimidating, but it's just too cute. When someone pats it on the head, it drops the tough-guy act and grins.

SPRITZEE
Perfume Pokémon

How to Say It: SPRIT-zee

Height: 0′ 08″

Weight: 1.1 lbs.

Possible Moves: Sweet Scent, Fairy Wind, Sweet Kiss, Odor Sleuth, Echoed Voice, Calm Mind, Draining Kiss, Aromatherapy, Attract, Moonblast, Charm, Flail, Misty Terrain, Skill Swap, Psychic, Disarming Voice

TYPE:
FAIRY

Long ago, this Pokémon was popular among the nobility for its lovely scent. Instead of spraying perfume, ladies would keep a Spritzee close at hand.

SWIRLIX

Cotton Candy Pokémon

How to Say It: SWUR-licks

Height: 1′ 04″

Weight: 7.7 lbs.

Possible Moves: Sweet Scent, Tackle, Fairy Wind, Play Nice, Fake Tears, Round, Cotton Spore, Endeavor, Aromatherapy, Draining Kiss, Energy Ball, Cotton Guard, Wish, Play Rough, Light Screen, Safeguard

TYPE:
FAIRY

Swirlix loves to snack on sweets. Its sugary eating habits have made its white fur sweet and sticky, just like cotton candy.

TAKE THE KALOS QUIZ!

Are you ready to prove you're a Pokémon expert? It's time to show that you're in the know. Put your knowledge of Kalos to the test by answering these twelve questions. Then turn the page to see if you made the grade.

1. Which Pokémon doesn't need a helmet because its head already has a hard shell protecting it? _____

2. What category of Pokémon is Froakie?
   _____

3. What's black and white, and always has a leaf in its teeth? _____

4. What Pokémon looks so much like candy you might think you can eat it? _____

5. Where does Helioptile get all its power?
   _____

6. Which Pokémon has been used as a perfume?
   _____

7. What special gift do a Gogoat's horns have?
    _____

8. Name two Pokémon in this book who give off heat during battle.
    _____

9. What Pokémon did Sylveon evolve from?
    _____

10. What new Pokémon type is found in Kalos?
    _____

11. Xerneas and Yveltal are Legendary Pokémon whose species represent what two forces?
    _____

12. What is always by Flabébé's side? _____
    _____

ANSWER KEY

1. Chespin
2. The Bubble Frog Pokémon
3. Pancham
4. Swirlix
5. From the sun
6. Spritzee
7. They can read their riders' feelings.
8. Fennekin and Litleo
9. Eevee
10. Fairy
11. Life and destruction
12. A flower

9-12 Correct Answers

Congratulations! When it comes to the Pokémon in Kalos, you're an expert! You pay close attention to your Pokémon, and any would be lucky to call you its Trainer.

5-8 Correct Answers

Way to go! You've shown you know your stuff and have what it takes to become an awesome Pokémon Trainer.

0-4 Correct Answers

You missed a few details along the way, but the good news is, it looks like there's plenty more fun for you to have with this book. Start at the beginning and get ready for another round with your favorite new Pokémon!